WHODUNITS?™

The Monster Mystery

Written by Jack Long
Illustrated by Leonard Shortall

Modern Publishing
A Division of Unisystems, Inc.
New York, New York 10022

TO AMANDA AND
STEPHEN - SHORTALL
L. S.

TO MY GRANDCHILD
NICHOLAS
C.D.L.

TO NINA AND JACK
RIESMAN
J. L.

Published by Modern Publishing,
a division of Unisystems, Inc.

Copyright © 1989 by Carlo DeLucia

TM—WHODUNITS? Mystery Storybooks is a trademark of Modern
Publishing, a division of Unisystems, Inc.

®—Honey Bear Books is a trademark of Honey Bear
Productions, Inc., and is registered in the U.S. Patent and
Trademark Office.

Printed in Belgium

TABLE OF CONTENTS

Chapter One
Teensy-Weensies

Knock–knock–knock!
Perry Possum opened the door of the Betty Beaver Detective Agency.

"Who is it, Perry?" Betty asked her able assistant.

"It's the Teensy-Weensies," Perry replied.

The Teensy-Weensies stepped into the agency—Little Susie Squirrel, Junior Chipmunk, Tiny Mouse, and Billy Bunny the Eleventh. The Teensy-Weensies were the Good Forest babies.

"We desperately need your help, Miss
Betty," said Little Susie Squirrel.

"Dethperately!" echoed Tiny Mouse, who
had a bit of a lisp.

11

"What's wrong?" asked Betty.
"There's a monster in Good Forest!" cried
Junior Chipmunk.

"A monster! What does it look like?" asked
Perry.

"It's very, very big," said Billy Bunny the Eleventh.

"It has a big mouth," continued Junior, as all the Good Forest babies tried to show Betty and Perry just how big it was.

"And it ith eating it'th way through Good Foretht," shrieked Tiny.

"I think we should take a look," Betty said
to Perry.

Perry hung the "Closed" sign on the agency door, and off they went deep into the forest with the Good Forest babies right behind them.

Suddenly, Junior shouted, "There it is!"

"Oooh—Oooh!" shrieked Tiny. He was
scared.
    Betty and Perry looked.

19

"Why it's a bulldozer!" Betty cried. "Come here, children! A bulldozer is a machine used to dig ditches and pull up trees and bushes. It's useful. It's not a monster."

"This one is!" cried Billy Bunny the Eleventh.
"Why do you say that?" asked Perry.
"Because," said Billy. "This one is eating
its way through Good Forest! Look over there!"

Betty and Perry looked again. They saw a wide path cut at the edge of the forest. All the trees and bushes that once grew there were pushed to one side.

"You're right," said Betty. "This doesn't look like the work of a useful machine. This looks like the work of someone or something that wants to destroy Good Forest!"

Chapter Two
At the Library

Betty and Perry told the Teensy-Weensies
to go home, while they set about trying to solve
the mystery.

"We'd better head to the library," Betty
said to Perry, "so that we can read up on
bulldozers."

Ophelia Owl, head librarian, was eager to help Betty and Perry.

"We keep our bulldozer books in this
section," she told them, leading them through
the tall shelves.

27

"Oh, my!" cried Ophelia Owl, pointing to an empty space on a shelf. "All the bulldozer books have been borrowed! How odd!"

"Do you know who might have borrowed them?" asked Perry.

"I'll check our file catalog," said Ophelia
Owl, as they walked back to the front desk.

"Let's see …" said Ophelia. "Hubert
Hedgehog, Ralph Raccoon, and Orson Otter
each took out one bulldozer book. Mike Moose
took out the other three."

"Well," Betty said. "I know Hubert, Ralph and Orson very well. I doubt any of them would misuse a bulldozer."

"Still," she said. "We must question them."
"And then we must talk to Mike Moose,"
said Perry. "I wonder who he is. I've
never heard of him."

"Neither have I," said Ophelia Owl.

"I don't know who he is either," said Betty.
"But we're going to find out!"

Chapter Three
Who's Mike Moose?

Betty and Perry went to see Hubert Hedgehog. Hubert was a house builder.

"I use bulldozers when I build houses," said Hubert. "So I took out a book to read more about them. But I never used one to harm Good Forest."

"Thank you," said Betty. "We believe you, Hubert."

Ralph Raccoon said he used bulldozers to build roads.

"I took out a book to read up on bulldozer safety," he said. "Not so I could use one to destroy anything!"

"That's what we thought," said Betty.
"Thanks for answering our questions."

Orson Otter also said he would never use a
bulldozer to hurt Good Forest. "I'm a ditch
digger," Orson explained. "I read about all
kinds of machines. The books teach me a lot."

"Well," Betty said to Perry. "That leaves
Mike Moose!"

Betty and Perry set off for the mayor's
house.

They wanted to ask the mayor if she knew who the mysterious Mike Moose was and where he lived.

"Of course I know Mike Moose," said
Mayor Mildred Muskrat. "I was the one who
asked him to come live in Good Forest."

"Why?" asked Perry.

"To be our forest ranger," said the mayor.

"Mike lives in the forest ranger tower in the middle of Good Forest," Mayor Mildred told them.

Betty and Perry set off for the forest ranger tower.

"The mayor seems to trust Mike Moose not to do anything wrong like we trust Hubert and Ralph and Orson," said Perry.

"I know," Betty said. "But we still have to talk to him."

Perry knocked on the tower door.
The door opened.
"Are you Mike Moose?" asked Betty.

"Yes," said Mike Moose. "And you must be
Betty Beaver, the detective, and Perry Possum,
her able assistant. Mayor Mildred Muskrat has
told me a lot about you."

"We'd like to ask you a few questions,"
said Betty, as they followed Mike inside.
"Go right ahead," said Mike.

Over milk and cookies, Betty and Perry
explained the situation to Mike.
"Come look out of the tower window," said
Mike. "I'll explain everything."

"There's the path you are talking about," Mike said. "And yes, I cut it. But it's not a bad thing."

"That path is called a fire line," Mike said. "If a fire started outside of Good Forest, there's a good chance it would stop at the edge of that path, and not go into the forest."

"Why?" asked Perry as he looked through the telescope.

"Because," Mike said, "there wouldn't be any bushes or trees in that area to burn up."

"So the fire line helps protect us from forest fires!" Betty smiled.
"That's right!" said Mike.

Betty and Perry were relieved and asked
Mike to come with them through Good Forest
to meet the Teensy-Weensies and all his new
neighbors.

Everyone in Good Forest was glad to meet
their new forest ranger.

"The monster mystery is solved," Perry
sighed happily. "And we have a new friend."

"That's right," said Betty. "One who's going to keep us all fired up about learning the rules of forest safety."